A Note from Michelle about The Substitute Teacher

Hi! I'm Michelle Tanner. I'm nine years old. The worst thing just happened to me. I got caught playing a prank on my substitute teacher.

And do you know what he did? He put *me* in charge of teaching the class! Can you believe it?

And then after that, I had to tutor a bunch of second-graders. At least my family volunteered to help me with my lesson plans. And that means a lot of help—because I have a very big family!

There's my dad and my two older sisters, D.J. and Stephanie. But that's not all.

My mom died when I was little. So my uncle Jesse moved in to help Dad take care of us. So did Joey Gladstone. He's my dad's friend from college. It's almost like having three dads. But that's still not all!

First Uncle Jesse got married to Becky Donaldson. Then they had twin boys, Nicky and Alex. The twins are four years old now. And they're so cute.

That's nine people. Our dog, Comet, makes ten. Sure it gets kind of crazy sometimes. But I wouldn't change it for anything. It's so much fun living in a full house!

FULL HOUSE™ MICHELLE novels

The Great Pet Project
The Super-Duper Sleepover Party
My Two Best Friends
Lucky, Lucky Day
The Ghost in My Closet
Ballet Surprise
Major League Trouble
My Fourth-Grade Mess
Bunk 3, Teddy and Me
My Best Friend Is a Movie Star!
The Big Turkey Escape
The Substitute Teacher
Calling All Planets
I've Got a Secret
How to Be Cool

Available from MINSTREL Books

FULL HOUSE™
Michelle

The Substitute Teacher

Cathy East Dubowski

A Parachute Press Book

R E A D I N G

A MINSTREL® BOOK

Published by POCKET BOOKS
New York   London   Toronto   Sydney   Tokyo   Singapore

A MINSTREL PAPERBACK *Original*

A Minstrel Book published by
POCKET BOOKS, a division of Simon & Schuster Inc.
1230 Avenue of the Americas, New York, NY 10020

A PARACHUTE PRESS BOOK

READING Copyright © and ™ 1997 by Warner Bros.

FULL HOUSE, characters, names and all related indicia are trademarks of Warner Bros. © 1997.

ISBN: 0-671-00364-X

First Minstrel Books printing January 1997

10   9   8   7   6   5   4

A MINSTREL BOOK and colophon are registered trademarks of Simon & Schuster Inc.

Cover photo by Schultz Photography

Printed in the U.S.A.

Chapter

1

♥ "I don't want to go to school tomorrow!" nine-year-old Michelle Tanner said, pouting.

She loaded another plate into the dishwasher. And I don't want to do the dishes tonight, she thought. In Michelle's full house, after-dinner cleanup was a super-big job!

Nine people lived in the big Tanner house. Her dad, her eighteen-year-old sister D.J., and her thirteen-year-old sister Stephanie. Plus her uncle Jesse, his wife,

Becky, and their four-year-old twins, Nicky and Alex. They lived up on the third floor.

And her dad's friend from college, Joey Gladstone, lived downstairs. Joey and Jesse both moved in a long time ago—right after Michelle's mother died.

Nine people make a lot of dirty dishes, Michelle thought. At least I don't have to wash Comet's bowl. He licks it absolutely clean.

And she didn't have to scrub the pots and pans: That was Joey's job tonight. She didn't have to clear the table either: It was Uncle Jesse's turn for that chore.

Michelle's dad glanced over at her. "Michelle! Why don't you want to go to school? I thought you loved Mrs. Yoshida's class." Danny smoothed a sheet of foil around half a loaf of pumpkin bread.

"I do like school," Michelle answered. "But Mrs. Yoshida won't be there tomor-

2

row. She left school early to rush to the hospital."

"Oh, no!" Danny exclaimed. "What happened?"

"Is she all right?" Jesse cried.

"She's fine. Her sister was having her baby, and Mrs. Yoshida wanted to be there," Michelle explained. "She's not going to be in school tomorrow, so she can help her sister and the baby get settled."

"That's a relief," Joey said.

"Mrs. Yoshida is the best teacher I ever had. School will be totally rotten without her! If she's not going to be there—I don't want to be there either," Michelle complained.

"Don't worry, honey," her father said. He carried the leftovers to the refrigerator. "You'll probably have a very nice substitute teacher while she's gone."

Michelle wrinkled her nose. "The last time I had a substitute was in the third grade. Mrs. Dowling. She was awful! She used to be a school nurse. She made us do work sheets about Terry Tooth and Count Cavity. She treated us like babies!"

"Now, Michelle," Danny said. "Not all substitutes are awful."

Michelle rolled her eyes and sighed. She could tell her dad didn't really understand. "I guess you're right," she answered.

"You pots and pans can't escape me!" Joey shouted as he splashed in the sudsy water. Soap bubbles clung to his sandy blond hair and his wild Hawaiian-print shirt. He even had foam on his chin. "I'm the meanest pirate to sail the dirty dishwater—Captain Bubblebeard!"

Jesse snorted as he handed Michelle three more plates to load.

"Uh, excuse me, Captain," Danny called out. "I believe the idea here is to clean up—not mess up!"

Michelle giggled. My dad, the neat

freak, she thought. It's funny that he's best friends with Joey—when Joey can be such a slob.

"Aye, aye, Captain Clean!" Joey laughed as he wiped up the counter.

Danny shook his head. "Well, I've got some reading to do for work. I'll be upstairs if you need me." He left the kitchen.

"Hey, Michelle!" Joey said with a twinkle in his eye. "You know what I used to do when I had a substitute?"

"What?" Michelle asked.

"Play sink the sub!" Joey cried. He dove his orange scrubby pad into the sink, pretending it was a submarine.

Michelle shook her head. "I don't get it."

"Sub isn't short just for submarine," Joey told her. "It's also short for substitute teacher. Get it?"

Jesse brought some more plates to the counter. He shook his long black hair out

5

of his eyes. "Oh, man. You wouldn't believe what my friends and I used to do when we had subs—"

"*We* always switched names," Joey said.

"That's beginner stuff," Jesse replied. "One time my best friend pretended he couldn't speak English. He made up his own funny language."

"We did something better," Joey bragged. "Once we put a big fake spider in the substitute's bottom drawer. I tied a string to its leg. We waited and waited till she opened that drawer. Then I jerked the string, and the spider jumped out."

Jesse hooted with laughter. "Cool!" Michelle exclaimed.

"It didn't even look real!" Joey continued. "We tried to tell the sub it wasn't. But she wouldn't believe us. She jumped up on her desk and wouldn't come down until the principal came to rescue her."

Nobody did anything like that to Mrs. Dowling! Michelle thought.

"We got in trouble for that. Big trouble," Joey finished. "The principal made us all stay after class, and we each had to write the sub a letter to apologize."

"Yeah, now those tricks seem pretty silly," Jesse added.

Michelle rinsed the last plate and stuck it in the dishwasher. She shut the door and turned the knob to start the wash cycle.

"I'm going upstairs," she announced to Jesse and Joey. Then she ran up to the bedroom she shared with Stephanie.

She found Stephanie sprawled on her stomach on her bed. Her long blond ponytail hung over her shoulder and brushed her notebook. She put her finger to her lips. "Shhh! I'm concentrating."

"Okay, okay," Michelle said.

Michelle had finished her homework that afternoon. So she dug her special

7

scented markers out of the bottom drawer. She found a piece of stiff white paper and some colored glitter.

Now I have everything I need to make a welcome back card for Mrs. Yoshida, she thought. When she comes back to school, I want her to know how great I think she is.

Michelle worked on the card for more than an hour. "Steph, look," she called when she finished. She held up the card so her sister could read it. It said:

To the Best Teacher in the World!
Welcome back, Mrs. Yoshida!
We missed you!
Love, Michelle

"Uh-huh," Stephanie mumbled. She shot a glance at the card. "That's nice."

"It smells good too." Michelle put away her scented magic markers and the rest of her art supplies. She plopped down on her bed and leaned back against her pink and blue pillows.

Tomorrow she would spend the whole day with some stranger—a teacher she had never met before. Michelle brushed her strawberry-blond bangs out of her eyes and thought about Mrs. Dowling. Ugh!

She still remembered how Mrs. Dowling embarrassed her in front of the whole class. It happened when she took attendance.

"Michelle Tanner!" Mrs. Dowling exclaimed. "I have the sweetest, most darling little toy poodle named Michelle. She has blond hair—just like yours."

"Any relation, Michelle?" her friend Jeff Farrington joked.

Kids started barking every time they saw her. And they didn't stop for weeks!

Michelle's face felt hot as she thought about it.

She sighed. Maybe the substitute

teacher they got tomorrow would be okay. Maybe she wouldn't do anything to embarrass Michelle.

But she would be so happy when it was time to give Mrs. Yoshida her welcome back card!

Chapter 2

♥ "What's going on?" Michelle asked as she joined a group of her friends on the playground the next morning.

"Everybody's talking about the substitute teacher we're going to have," her best friend, Mandy Metz, explained.

"Nobody has seen her yet," Michelle's other best friend, Cassie Wilkins, told her. "Our classroom is empty."

"Maybe they couldn't find anybody to take our class," their friend Lee Wagner said.

"Oh, no!" Jeff Farrington joked, clutching his head. "You mean I did all my homework for nothing?"

Michelle laughed. Jeff reminded her of Joey, always kidding around. Maybe he would grow up to be a comedian too.

"I hope we don't get Mrs. Dowling!" Michelle exclaimed.

"Eww! Me too," Anna Abdul agreed. "I had her once. All she ever talks about is teeth and germs and her *darling* little poodle."

Michelle held her breath. No one seemed to remember that the little poodle's name was Michelle.

"Have you ever heard of sink the sub?" Michelle asked her friends.

"Uhn-uh. What is it?" Cassie asked.

Michelle told them about the tricks Joey and Jesse used to play on subs. Everyone laughed.

"We have to play sink the sub too!" Jeff cried. "Let's hurry up and make plans."

"Wait a minute!" Michelle interrupted. "I didn't mean we should do anything. Joey and Jesse got in big trouble for tricking their subs."

"It's no big deal. My sister and her friends always play jokes on substitutes," Anna announced. She took off her red hairband, smoothed down her shiny brown hair, and slid the hairband back on.

"Substitutes expect it," Jeff said. "We don't want to hurt our sub's feelings, do we?"

"Oh, right!" Cassie said. "My feelings would be *soooo* hurt if no one put a fake bug in my desk."

"If it gets us out of some work, I'm for it," Lee chimed in.

Jeff slapped Lee a high five.

"I think switching names would be fun," Mandy added. "And it won't scare the substitute or anything. The sub never even has to find out!"

"I'll switch with you," Cassie volunteered.

Jeff and Lee decided to switch names. And Michelle agreed to switch names with Anna.

The bell rang.

Here we go! Michelle thought. She grabbed her backpack and followed the others into their classroom.

The teacher's desk was still empty.

"Maybe they really couldn't find anybody," Mandy said.

"All right!" Jeff exclaimed. He pumped his fist in the air. "Kids rule!"

"Bad news," Michelle told Mandy. "If they had this much trouble finding somebody, our sub will be the worst."

Two kids started playing ticktacktoe on the chalkboard. Lee pulled out his new action figure and showed it to Jeff. Cassie,

Mandy, and Michelle huddled in one corner, discussing what to do on Saturday. Rollerblading or the new science fiction movie?

A tall, thin woman burst into the room. "Students—students! Sit down this instant!"

"Miss Strickland," Michelle whispered. She rushed to her desk and slid into the seat. She kept her eyes on the floor.

Everyone was afraid of Miss Strickland. She taught the second-grade class across the hall. Miss *Strict*-land the kids called her behind her back.

"What in the world is going on in here?" Miss Strickland demanded. "I could hear you all the way in my classroom!"

Michelle glanced up and found Miss Strickland staring at the empty teacher's desk. "Um-hmn!"

Then Michelle heard footsteps running

down the hall. Sneakers squeaked on the tile floor, and a young blond guy slid to a stop outside the classroom.

Who is he? Michelle wondered. His face glowed a bright red. His hair stood up on one side. And his tie had flipped over his shoulder.

"Hey, somebody's big brother is here!" Jeff called out. "Who forgot their lunch?"

"Hmph!" Miss Strickland snorted.

The guy at the door smoothed down his hair and straightened his tie. He rubbed his hands nervously on his jeans. Then he walked into the classroom. "Hi. I'm Joe Kowalski—your substitute teacher."

That's our sub? Michelle thought. He doesn't look much older than D.J.!

Miss Strickland appeared shocked. Michelle didn't blame her.

"Sorry I'm a little late," Mr. Kowalski told them, his face still red.

Miss Strickland looked up at the clock

on the wall. "Teachers should set a good example for their students," she said firmly. Then she turned and hurried back across the hall to her class. She kept her shoulders back and her chin up.

Mr. Kowalski stared after her for a moment. "Good morning to you too," he mumbled.

He wrote his name on the board. Then he turned around and smiled at the class. Michelle thought he seemed a little nervous.

"I have a secret to share with you," he said. "This is my first time as a substitute teacher. So I need all of you to help me out. Okay?"

Jeff turned around in his seat. "Excellent!" he whispered. "He'll be easy to fool!"

Michelle felt a little bad for Mr. Kowalski. Maybe they shouldn't play tricks on him—not on his very first day.

"Okay, so let's get started," Mr. Kowalski said. He picked up Mrs. Yoshida's attendance book and flipped through it. "Uh, I think there should be a seating chart in here. One second and I'll find it."

A crumpled piece of paper landed on Michelle's desk. She glanced at Mr. Kowalski. He was still busy, so Michelle smoothed the paper out.

It was a note from Jeff. It said: *I have the seating chart. Ha-ha!*

"I'll make a chart as we go," Mr. Kowalski said. "Okay. Roll call. First name. Anna Abdul."

Michelle swallowed hard. She and Anna exchanged glances. Should I do it? Michelle thought.

"Is Anna here?" Mr. Kowalski asked.

Why do I have to go first, Michelle thought. What if no one switches but Anna and me?

All the kids in the class stared at Michelle and Anna. She heard a few giggles and whispers.

Oh, why didn't I switch names with Heather Zimmerman! Michelle thought. Or Cassie—she's a "W." Then it wouldn't all be up to me.

Someone poked her in the ribs.

"Go on!" Jeff whispered. "Do it!"

Chapter 3

♥ "Anna Abdul?" Mr. Kowalski called one more time.

Jeff tapped Michelle on the head. "Anna, you are spacing out again! Didn't you hear Mr. K. call your name?"

"Here," Michelle answered.

Mr. Kowalski smiled at her and checked off her name. "That's okay, Anna. I space out sometimes too."

Michelle heard Mandy give a loud snort. Jeff started to cough—to cover up his burst of laughter. Lee gave Michelle the thumbs-up sign.

Michelle peeked at Mr. Kowalski. Did he see the thumbs-up? Did he know kids were laughing at him? What would he do if he found out she wasn't really Anna?

"Jonathan Bennett?" Mr. Kowalski called out. The wrong kid answered.

Whew! Michelle let out a big breath of air. She felt more and more relaxed as each kid answered to the wrong name.

It's just for today, she told herself. Mrs. Yoshida will be here tomorrow, and everything will be back to normal.

"Michelle Tanner."

Michelle jumped when she heard Mr. Kowalski call her name. She locked her teeth together to keep from answering. I'm not Michelle Tanner today, she reminded herself. I'm Anna. Anna Abdul.

"Oh, good," Mr. Kowalski said when Anna raised her hand. "Mrs. Yoshida left me a special note. She said I should be sure to ask Michelle Tanner if I needed anything, because Michelle is friendly, helpful, and she knows where everything is."

Mrs. Yoshida wrote that about me? Michelle thought. Wow! How cool!

Then she started to feel a little bad. Mrs. Yoshida trusted her to help the sub—and she was playing a trick on him!

I wish we hadn't switched names, Michelle thought. Mrs. Yoshida wrote great stuff about me, and I can't even enjoy it. And it might have been fun to help Mr. Kowalski.

"All right," Mr. Kowalski said when he finished taking attendance. "We have a spelling test scheduled this morning. Good. I like spelling." He grinned at them. "With a name like Kowalski, you have to be a good speller."

Michelle liked spelling too. She even liked spelling tests.

"Everyone take out a clean sheet of

paper, please," Mr. Kowalski said. He strolled past Jeff's desk and shut his spelling book. "Better put that away."

"But Mrs. Yoshida always lets us use our books for tests," Jeff complained.

Michelle bit the inside of her cheek to keep from laughing. It might be Mr. Kowalski's first day, but no one was dumb enough to believe that!

Mr. Kowalski grinned. "Good try. Now please put your book away."

Jeff shrugged and stuck the book inside his desk.

"Ready?" Mr. Kowalski asked. "The first word is—"

Snap!

"Mr. K.!" Jeff called out, waving his hand in the air. "I just broke my pencil! Can I sharpen it?"

"Yes, um . . ." Mr. Kowalski checked his new seating chart. "Lee."

Everyone giggled when Mr. Kowalski called Jeff by the wrong name.

Jeff dashed to the sharpener. Michelle saw him wink at Lee on the way.

Snap! Lee broke his pencil on the corner of his desk. "May I sharpen my pencil too?" Lee asked.

Mr. Kowalski nodded. "Just hurry up, please."

Snap! Snap! Snap!

Pencils broke all over the room.

Michelle grinned. She pushed down on her pencil. *Snap!* The point broke. She jumped up and joined the long line of kids waiting to use the sharpener.

Lee stopped next to her on the way back to his desk. "Hey *Anna,*" he whispered. "Does your watch have a beeper?"

"It has everything." Michelle loved the pink wristwatch her dad gave her. It showed the time in London, Tokyo, Los Angeles, and New York. It gave the date.

She could use it as a stopwatch—or a compass! She could even enter special phone numbers and reminders into its memory. All her friends thought it was so cool.

"Let me borrow it," Lee said. "I just thought of a great joke."

"Keep the line moving," Mr. Kowalski called out. "Mrs. Yoshida left us a lot of work to get through today."

Michelle slipped off the watch and handed it to Lee. "Be careful with it," she instructed. "It was a present from my dad."

A few minutes later, she was back at her desk, ready for the first word of the spelling test. Michelle felt confident. She studied hard—and spelling was her best subject.

Michelle began to write her name in the top right-hand corner of her paper. M-I-C-H-

"Psst! You have to write Anna Abdul," Jeff warned her.

Oh, no! Michelle hadn't thought about using Anna's name on a test. What if Anna didn't study? Michelle didn't want to get a bad grade because of her.

She glanced around the room. Was everyone else using their fake name?

"Hey, Mr. K.! Does it count against us if we misspell our names?" Jeff joked.

Michelle noticed a few kids start erasing. Anna twisted around in her seat and nodded at Michelle.

This stinks! Michelle thought. I want to put my own name on the test. But I'll get everybody in trouble if I do.

Slowly Michelle erased M-I-C-H. Then she sighed and wrote Anna Abdul at the top of her paper.

Mr. Kowalski called out the first word. I hope Anna is a good speller, Michelle thought.

Michelle had received a perfect grade on every single spelling test so far. If she could keep it up until the end of the year, her dad promised her a special day in the city—just the two of them!

She loved going to Fisherman's Wharf and the wax museum, and riding on the cable cars.

But if Anna wasn't a good speller—Michelle could forget about her special day right now!

Chapter 4

♥ "Please pass your tests forward," Mr. Kowalski said.

Beep-beep! Beep-beep! Beep-beep!

"What's that?" the sub asked.

"Recess bell!" Lee called. He jumped up and hurried toward the door, Jeff right behind him.

"Wait!" Mr. Kowalski ordered. He crossed the room and stared out the window at the playground. "None of the other classes are out there," he said.

Beep-beep! Beep-beep! Beep-beep!

"Each class has its own recess time," Jeff explained. "That's why the bell is so soft. It doesn't disturb the other classes."

Mr. Kowalski looked doubtful.

Should I tell him the truth? Michelle wondered.

"Really, Mr. Kowalski!" Cassie piped up. "We always have the first recess!"

Beep-beep! Beep-beep! Beep-beep!

"Okay, everyone. Make a single line and head out to the playground," Mr. Kowalski instructed.

Michelle joined the line. She didn't know what else to do. It's no big deal, she told herself. We're not really hurting anything.

Mandy scooted in line behind her. "We could be in big trouble for this," she said in Michelle's ear.

Miss Strickland stormed out of her room and glared at Mr. Kowalski. "What is going on out here? Why is your class in the hall? What is all this noise?" she demanded.

"Recess?" Mr. Kowalski answered. He sounded a little nervous.

The hall fell silent.

Did Mandy say *big* trouble? Michelle thought. How about *super-size triple trouble?*

Miss Strickland folded her arms. "Recess? At ten in the morning?" She peered over her glasses at Mr. Kowalski. Then she studied the face of every kid.

Michelle felt her cheeks grow hot when Miss Strickland stared at her. She can't read your mind, Michelle reminded herself. But she didn't feel absolutely sure.

Mr. Kowalski turned toward the class. "Okay, I get it. I used to be a kid too, you know."

His face was red. And he looked angry. Really angry.

Michelle stared down at the floor. She

felt too embarrassed to meet Mr. Kowalski's eyes.

I wish we hadn't made him look bad, she thought. Especially on his very first day.

Mr. Kowalski cleared his throat. "Um, I think my students are having a little fun with the substitute."

"There is only one way to deal with a class that is out of control," Miss Strickland said.

Michelle couldn't believe it. Miss Strickland was lecturing Mr. Kowalski as if *he* were a fourth-grader.

"You have to be tough," Miss Strickland said. "You have to be strict! Whoever pulled this prank should be marched straight to the principal's office."

The principal's office! Michelle had never been sent to the principal's office!

She held her breath. What if Mr. Kowalski found out it was her watch beeping.

What would he do? Would she have to go to the principal's office?

"Thank you for your advice," Mr. Kowalski told Miss Strickland as she returned to her class.

Mr. Kowalski didn't say another word. He walked back to their classroom, opened the door, and pointed inside.

This is worse than being yelled at, Michelle thought. If he yelled, at least we would know what he's thinking. And what he plans to do.

She and her friends exchanged nervous glances as they filed back into the classroom and took their seats.

Everyone sat perfectly still. Michelle's beeping watch was the only sound.

Mr. Kowalski tracked the beeping to a bookshelf near the window. He reached behind a box of tissues. Then he pulled out the watch and turned off the beeper.

He walked up and down the rows of

desks with the pink watch in his hand.
"Now, whose is this?"

Michelle opened her mouth—but nothing came out. She shot a look at Lee.
Would he speak up?

"It's not my watch," Lee whispered to
her.

Mr. Kowalski sighed as he returned to
the front of the room. "Okay," he said.
"Maybe we should see how many kids can
fit into the principal's office at one time—"

"It's Michelle's watch!" Anna blurted
out.

Just as Michelle called out "It's mine!"

"What?" Mr. Kowalski exclaimed. He
stared from Anna to Michelle. "Whom
does this watch belong to?"

Great. The two girls gazed at each other.
Now what should they do?

Michelle swallowed hard. "I'm Michelle
Tanner, not Anna Abdul," she admitted.

"We switched names—just for fun. The watch is mine."

"Would you come up front, please," Mr. Kowalski asked.

Michelle's heart pounded as she stood and started toward Mr. Kowalski's desk.

"Wait!" Lee cried. "It *is* Michelle's watch. But I turned on the beeper."

Mr. Kowalski turned to Michelle. "Did he steal your watch?"

"No," Michelle mumbled. "I gave it to him." Why did she ever think it would be fun to sink the sub?

"Did you know what he planned to do with it?" Mr. Kowalski asked.

Michelle hesitated. "Not exactly . . . but, well, sort of," she said. She couldn't blame the whole thing on Lee. She knew he planned to play a trick on their sub with her watch—and she still let him borrow it.

"I think you'd better join Michelle up here, Jeff," Mr. Kowalski told Lee.

Lee shuffled over to Michelle. "Uh—my name's not Jeff," he mumbled. "It's Lee."

Mr. Kowalski dragged another chair behind the teacher's desk. "Have a seat," he told them.

Huh? Michelle thought. She sat down in one of the chairs. Isn't he going to send us to the principal?

"It's obvious you don't like my teaching—so I quit," Mr. Kowalski announced.

Mandy gasped.

"Whoa," Lee muttered.

We sank the sub! Michelle thought. She couldn't believe it! What would Mrs. Yoshida say?

Mr. Kowalski took off his tie. He unbuttoned the top button of his shirt. "I must need to learn more about the fourth grade—so I'm joining the class."

"This is a joke, right?" Jeff called out.

"No joke," Mr. Kowalski answered.

"But who's going to be our teacher?" Heather asked. She sounded worried.

Mr. Kowalski grinned. "Let me introduce you to your new substitute teachers."

Oh, no, Michelle thought. Her heart began to pound. He couldn't. He wouldn't.

Mr. Kowalski plopped down in Michelle's chair. His long legs sprawled into the aisle.

"Miss Tanner," he said cheerfully. "Mr. Wagner. The class is all yours!"

Chapter
5

♥ "Me . . . and Lee . . . the teachers!" Michelle exclaimed. She glanced around the room. Everyone stared at them.

"That's right," Mr. Kowalski answered. "Go ahead. Teach us something. Unless you would rather go to the principal's office . . . ?"

"No!" Lee blurted out.

"We'll teach!" Michelle agreed.

Michelle gazed out at the class. Cassie smiled at her sympathetically. Mandy shrugged and shook her head. And Jeff had his hand clapped over his mouth—trying not to laugh.

"What should we do first?" Michelle whispered to Lee.

He didn't answer.

"You might try following Mrs. Yoshida's lesson plan," Mr. Kowalski called out. "It's right there on the corner of the desk."

Michelle picked it up. Her hands wouldn't stop shaking. The sheets of paper rustled as she tried to read them. Attendance. Spelling test. What came next?

"Hey, teacher," someone yelled in a high, squeaky voice. "You want these spelling tests back, or what?"

Michelle jerked her head up. Who said that?

Mr. Kowalski blew a huge bubble-gum bubble and popped it loudly.

Mr. Kowalski! What was he doing? He

should be setting a good example for the rest of the class.

Not if he wants to punish us, Michelle realized. She stood up straighter. If this is what it took to stay out of the principal's office—hey, she would do it!

"Students, please pass your spelling tests to the front," Michelle said firmly.

Lee cracked up.

Thanks a lot, Michelle thought. Lee was supposed to be *helping* her.

A paper airplane made out of a spelling test sailed across the room and boinked Michelle in the forehead.

"Cool!" Lee picked the plane up and tossed it back.

Michelle rolled her eyes. "Way to go, Lee."

Dozens more paper airplanes dive-bombed her. "Come on, you guys. Stop it!" she pleaded. She collected all the paper airplanes and piled them on one corner of the desk. She would sort them out later.

Michelle checked the lesson plan. Grammar next. Good. Most of the class hated grammar—and they deserved it. They were all acting like jerks.

"I'll write this sentence on the board," she told Lee. "You pass out the work sheets."

Lee shrugged. "Okay."

When Michelle began explaining the first grammar problem, Mr. Kowalski started snoring. Snoring loudly.

"You're very rude!" she exclaimed.

Mr. Kowalski's eyes popped open. "Well, you're very boring!" he shot back in a high voice Michelle knew was supposed to sound like hers.

The whole class cracked up. Michelle felt her face get hot. She didn't know what to do, so she turned back to the chalkboard to write another example.

Thud! Thud! Thud!

Now what? Michelle turned around. Mr. Kowalski was showing the class how to make a giant domino run—with their science books.

This class is totally out of control! Michelle thought. And it's all Mr. Kowalski's fault! He's acting like a big brat!

Michelle glanced at the clock. Oh, no! She'd been teaching for only fifteen minutes! I knew today was going to be horrible, she thought. But I didn't know it was going to be this kind of horrible!

It's not easy to teach a class, Michelle realized. Especially when you've got a troublemaker like Mr. K.!

Michelle blew her hair out of her face. She felt like giving up. But she wouldn't. No way. She returned to her grammar lesson.

A few minutes later she caught Mr. Kowalski passing a note to Lee. Michelle marched over and snatched the note away. "Maybe you would like to share that with the rest of the class."

She unfolded the paper and found a goofy picture of a bunny wearing a chef's hat. A little cartoon bubble over its head said "Do you know the recipe for water?"

Michelle started to crumple the picture up. But Mr. Kowalski grabbed it away and held it up so everyone could see it.

"That's not funny," Cassie said. But she couldn't stop smiling.

Michelle felt tears burn her eyes. No one would listen to her.

No. I am not going to cry, she told herself. And I am going to *teach* this class.

Michelle remembered how she used to think it would be fun to be a teacher like Mrs. Yoshida. Now she knew she was wrong. Really wrong.

Mrs. Yoshida, Michelle thought. *She* never let the class get out of control like this. What made her so special? What made her such a good teacher?

She doesn't just stand at the front of the room and talk to us, Michelle decided. She gets us involved. We're always *doing* something in Mrs. Yoshida's class.

Yes, Michelle thought. That's exactly what makes Mrs. Yoshida special.

Now I know exactly what to do!

Chapter
6

♥ "Listen up!" Michelle called. She scanned the classroom. She needed her first guinea pig. And she knew just who to pick. Mr. "Sink the Sub" himself—Jeff Farrington.

It was Jeff's big idea to sink Mr. Kowalski, she thought. So it's only fair that he share in her punishment.

"Jeff Farrington—come to the front, please," she called.

"What did I do?" he complained as he shuffled to her desk.

"Nothing—yet." Michelle handed Jeff the chalk. "But you're going to teach math today."

"Huh?"

"We're going to take turns being the teacher," Michelle explained. She picked up Mrs. Yoshida's lesson plans and pointed to the math section. "Fractions, Jeff."

Michelle knew math was not his best subject. But he had been working hard to do better.

"Ha-ha, Michelle. No way," Jeff said. "Mr. Kowalski made you the teacher. You teach." He started to sit back down.

Michelle grabbed him by the arm. "Did you know my sister Stephanie baby-sits your little brothers and sisters sometimes?" she asked softly.

"So?" Jeff shoved her hand away.

Michelle leaned close to him and whispered in his ear. "So they told her all

about your lucky underwear—the pair
with all the smiley—"

"I would be happy to teach math, Miss
Tanner," Jeff announced in a loud voice.

I thought you would, Michelle thought.

Jeff copied a fractions problem onto the
board. "Now, all you have to do— Wait a
minute." He erased the problem and
started over.

A couple of kids laughed.

"Maybe we should get this on video,"
Mr. Kowalski called out.

"Cut it out, will you?" Jeff snapped. Jeff
liked to joke around. But he didn't like to
be laughed at.

Good! Michelle thought. She wanted
each kid to find out what it felt like to
stand up in front of the class and try to
teach.

"Okay, everybody," Jeff said, a deter-
mined look on his face. "Fractions can be

hard. You can't do them halfway!" He grinned. "Get it? Fractions. *Half*way."

Mr. Kowalski laughed, and Jeff started to relax.

When the math lesson was finished, Michelle had Jeff pick a kid to teach social studies.

Suddenly, Michelle remembered Mr. Kowalski. She glanced over at him. He smiled and gave Michelle a wink.

She smiled back. He must think I'm doing a good job! And I am! she realized.

By the end of the day, the kids had finished everything on Mrs. Yoshida's lesson plan. Mr. Kowalski even helped out a little when somebody got stuck. And her friends seemed to have fun!

Michelle felt proud of herself. Maybe she would like to be a teacher someday after all.

She sneaked a peek at her pink watch.

Almost time for the bell. "Homework," she announced.

Lee read Mrs. Yoshida's notes. "Math book page sixty-three, problems one through fifteen."

"Plus," Michelle added, "an essay."

The class groaned. "Do we have to do what she says?" someone asked Mr. Kowalski. "Even for homework?"

"She's the teacher," he replied.

Michelle smiled and went on. "Please write a two-page essay on your favorite movie."

"Hey, that sounds like fun," Jonathan Bennett said.

The bell rang. Finally! Michelle thought. It's over! As she gathered up her books, a few kids told her she did a good job.

"See you tomorrow, Miss Tanner," Jeff teased. "What kind of apples do you like? Red? Green? Or wormy?"

"You did a good job today, Michelle,"

The Substitute Teacher

Mr. Kowalski said. He sounded proud of her. "You should think about becoming a teacher when you grow up."

"Thanks. It was tough at first—but I guess that makes us even, huh?" she asked.

"I guess it does," he answered.

"Well, it's been nice knowing you! Maybe you'll get to sub at our school again," Michelle said. Then she ran out to catch up with Cassie and Mandy.

"Michelle!" Cassie exclaimed. "You were fantastic! I never had such a great time at school."

Mandy nodded. "Today could have been a disaster. But you made it fun."

Michelle couldn't stop smiling as she walked in the door of the Tanner house late that afternoon. Her day started out rotten—but it ended great. She couldn't wait to tell her family what a good teacher she was!

Maybe Dad won't ask me *why* Mr. Kowalski picked me to teach the class, she thought. He wouldn't like that part of the story at all!

"Anybody home?" Michelle called out.

"I'm in here," Joey answered from the kitchen. Michelle hurried in—just in time to see him take a huge bite from a meatball sandwich. A glob of tomato sauce splashed onto the floor.

Michelle shook her head. Good thing Dad didn't see that, she thought. He loves his clean kitchen almost as much as he loves all of us!

"Guess what happened at school today!" Michelle exclaimed. "No, don't guess. You'll never guess. I'll have to tell you!"

Joey swallowed. Then he picked up a glass of milk from the counter and took a long drink. "I don't have time right now," he answered when he finished. "I'm substituting for another comic tonight and I'm late already. Wish me luck okay?"

He put his glass in the sink and popped the rest of the sandwich in his mouth.

"Good luck," Michelle said.

"I want to hear everything tomorrow," Joey mumbled through the food in his mouth. Then he rushed out the kitchen door. A second later Michelle heard the front door slam.

Michelle decided to go upstairs and visit Aunt Becky, Uncle Jesse, and the twins. They will be interested in hearing about the way I taught my class, she thought.

But as she climbed the first flight of stairs, the twins came barreling down. Aunt Becky and Uncle Jesse were right behind them.

"We're off to family night at Nicky and

Alex's preschool," Aunt Becky explained. "See you later, Michelle."

"Bye, Michelle!" the twins cried.

Michelle shook her head. Didn't *anyone* have time to hear about her amazing day? She continued up the stairs and headed down the hall.

D.J. opened the door to her room and rushed out. "Enjoy your pizza night," she said as she passed Michelle. "I'm going to the movies."

"Pizza night?" Michelle repeated.

"Yeah," D.J. answered without slowing down. "Dad has a meeting, and everyone else has plans too. So you and Stephanie are supposed to order pizza. She's having a couple friends over to study with her. I don't remember who."

Michelle sighed. She loved ordering from the take-out pizza place. Especially her favorite pineapple and mushroom pizza. But tonight she felt like talking.

She wandered back downstairs and plopped down on the couch. Comet trotted over and rested his nose on her knee. "Do *you* want to hear what happened at school today, Comet?" Michelle asked. Comet thumped his tail.

Michelle told the dog the whole story. Then she gave him a scratch behind the ears. "I was terrific! I think I should teach every day!"

She wouldn't have said that if she had known what the next three days would be like.

Chapter 7

She went over again what she had and propped it against the desk so that fell over and raised his nose in his sleep.

"Do you want to hear what happened at school today, Oscar?" Michelle asked. Oscar thumped his tail.

Michelle told the dog the whole story. When she gave him a scratch behind the ears. "It was terrible! I think I should teach everyday."

♥ The next day, Michelle hurried to school. She wanted to put her welcome back card on Mrs. Yoshida's desk first thing.

Michelle ran to her classroom—and skidded to a stop. What's he doing here?

"Hi, Michelle," Mr. Kowalski said.

"Uh—hi. What are you doing here? I mean, um, where is Mrs. Yoshida?" Michelle asked.

"Oh, her sister didn't have her baby yet. False alarm. So Mrs. Yoshida arranged to take off a few more days. The baby is due any minute." Mr. Kowalski winked. "Looks like you're stuck with me for the rest of the week."

Michelle bit her lip. "Oh. Do I have to be the teacher again?"

Mr. Kowalski laughed. "No, I think I'd better take over today. After all, I'm the one getting paid."

That's a relief, Michelle thought as she went to her seat. Yesterday was sort of fun—but she didn't want to teach every day! She wanted to be a regular kid again.

The bell rang and the other kids in Michelle's class trooped in. Most of them seemed happy to see Mr. Kowalski. If they had to have a sub, they wanted him.

Mr. Kowalski called roll, and this time everyone answered to the right name. Then he handed back the spelling tests.

Michelle eagerly reached for her paper. Hey! It said her name on top. But the handwriting was Anna Abdul's. And the grade was a seventy-five!

"What did I get?" Michelle asked Anna. Anna held up the paper so Michelle could see.

Yes! One hundred and eight! I even got all the bonus words, Michelle thought. And I still have my perfect spelling record.

But the paper had "Anna Abdul" written on top. *Anna* would get the perfect grade. Michelle would be stuck with a *seventy-five*.

It's not fair, she thought. I worked hard for that one hundred and eight. And now I've lost the chance for a special day with Dad! Whose stupid idea was this anyway?

Mine, she answered herself. With some help from Joey, Jesse, Lee, Jeff, and the rest of my friends.

"Mr. K., can't we get our real tests back?" Lee called out.

"No!" Jeff interrupted. "Keep them this way!"

"Switch them!" Lee cried.

Not hard to figure out which of them got a higher grade, Michelle thought.

"I don't know," Mr. Kowalski said. "I gave that test fair and square. Now you want me to fool around with the grades?"

"Pleeeeez!" several kids begged. Michelle begged the loudest.

"Let me think about it," Mr. Kowalski said.

I have to convince him to change our grades, Michelle thought.

"I have an announcement," Mr. Kowalski continued. "Miss Strickland asked me for some help. She has a few kids in her second-grade class who are having trouble with spelling. She needs a tutor—an older student to help them learn the spelling words for the test they are having on Friday afternoon. Anyone interested?"

Jeff's hand shot up. "I'll do it!"

"Great," Mr. Kowalski answered. "You

can start today. You'll need to meet with them during your lunch hour. I told Miss Strickland her kids could come to our room for the tutoring sessions—since the rest of our class will be at lunch."

Jeff raised his hand again. "Uh, Mr. K.? I just remembered. I'm a bad speller. You better get someone else to do it."

He wanted to do it only if he could get out of class, Michelle thought.

Mr. Kowalski glanced around the room. "Any other volunteers?"

No one answered.

"I'll make a deal with you," Mr. Kowalski said. "If someone helps the second-grade kids do better on Friday's test, I'll switch all your spelling grades."

"Michelle!" Lee called out.

"What?" Michelle exclaimed.

"Come on, Michelle," Lee begged. "You're the best speller in class. Everyone knows that. Come on. I'll trade lunches with you for a whole week!"

Michelle laughed. Every time she wanted Lee to do something for her she offered to trade lunches. Lee loved all the special goodies Danny packed for her.

"Oh, that's a great trade," Michelle joked. But if it took tutoring some little kids to get her 108 points back, she would do it.

"Looks like you're elected, Michelle," Mr. Kowalski said.

"All right, you three. I expect you to behave, and listen to Michelle," Miss Strickland said. She hurried back across the hall to her own classroom.

Michelle took a deep breath. "Let's get started. Why don't you tell me your names."

A boy with bright red hair and freckles

piped up. "I'm Robbie. And that's Alan and Claire."

All three kids stared at her. They look so sweet, Michelle thought. This is going to be easy! Spelling is my best subject. And I did a great job teaching yesterday—Mr. Kowalski said so.

"Robbie, can you spell *banana* for me?" Michelle asked.

Robbie ran to the board and grabbed some chalk.

Look how into the lesson he is, Michelle thought. He got up to the board in two seconds.

Robbie started to draw a superhero.

"No, Robbie. I want you to spell *banana*," Michelle called to him.

Robbie kept drawing. Alan dashed up beside him and drew a spaceship attacking Robbie's superhero.

Michelle jumped to her feet. "Robbie, Alan—this isn't recess time."

Alan banged two erasers together. "Kkrrrgh—Ka-BOOM!" he cried. "Gotcha!"

Yellow chalk dust filled the air.

Michelle sneezed. Did I say sweet? Wrong! "Boys"—*achoo!*—"sit down!"

The twins never acted this way when Michelle took care of them. But they were only four. Second-graders must be a lot different, Michelle thought.

Robbie jammed his hands on his hips and frowned at her. "We don't have to do what you say."

"Yes, you do!" Michelle shot back.

"No, we don't," Alan chimed in. He banged the erasers together again. "You're not our *real* teacher. We only have to do what our *real* teacher says."

"Well, you better sit down," Michelle snapped. "Or I'll tell your *real* teacher!"

"Aw, man!" Robbie slammed down the chalk and stomped back to his seat. Alan threw the erasers on the floor and followed him.

This is going to be harder than I thought, Michelle realized. Yesterday I was teaching kids my own age. Kids I knew. How am I going to get these three to listen?

Claire bounced up and down in her seat, her dark brown braids flying. "I know how to spell *banana!*" she cried. "Ask me! Ask me!"

Thank you, Claire, Michelle thought. At least one of the three kids wanted to try. "Great. Go ahead."

Claire scrunched up her face, thinking hard. "B-U-H . . . umm . . . N-A-N . . . N-U-H."

Whoa. These kids need a *lot* of help on their spelling. "That's a good try, Claire," Michelle began. "But it's not quite right. Let me give you a hint. There are no—"

Claire gave a snort of laughter. The boys cracked up.

Oh, I get it, Michelle thought angrily. Claire misspelled the word on purpose. Just to be funny! I can't believe I fell for that one!

"No, no, no!" Robbie called out. "It's B-U-Y-N-Z-L-S-Q!"

"No, it's not!" Alan cried. It's B-A-N-A-N-A-N-A-A-N-A!"

"Stop!" Michelle shouted.

The three kids shrieked with laughter.

What do I do? Michelle thought hopelessly. Then she remembered Miss Strickland. Kids didn't act up in *her* class. What did she say to Mr. Kowalski?

There is only one way to deal with a class that is out of control. You have to be tough. You have to be strict.

Maybe that is what it takes with kids like these, Michelle decided.

Michelle stood up straight and tall. She

glared at the kids, trying to make her face as scary as Miss Strickland's. "Children! Be quiet this instant!"

Alan covered his ears and hummed so he couldn't hear her. He squeezed his eyes shut so he couldn't see her scary face.

"I have to go to the bathroom!" Claire bellowed.

"Children! Be quiet this instant!" Robbie imitated Michelle. He twisted his own face into a stern, scary expression.

Michelle felt like screaming! Well, they aren't getting away with this, she thought. I'll show them!

She opened her notebook and started to write. Every few seconds she looked up and studied one of the kids, then wrote some more.

"What are you writing?" Claire finally asked.

"I'm writing down everything you do.

When Miss Strickland gets back, I'm going to give her my notes."

At first the kids looked scared. Good, Michelle thought. They deserve it.

"No, you won't," Robbie announced.

"Why not?" Michelle demanded.

"If you do, we'll tell Miss Strickland you were mean to us. We'll tell her you made Claire cry." He turned to Claire. "Go ahead. Show her."

Claire took a deep breath. Her bottom lip began to tremble. Her face scrunched up—and she burst into tears.

"Oh, no! Stop, stop, please stop!" Michelle begged. If she couldn't get Claire to stop crying, she wouldn't have time to go over all twenty words that would be on the test.

And if these kids aren't ready for their test on Friday afternoon, I will be stuck with a seventy-five on *my* test.

"Waaaa-*aaahhhhh!*" Claire wailed.

Michelle patted Claire on the shoulder. "Shhhhh, shhhh. I won't tell. I promise!"

Claire stopped crying instantly and grinned at the boys. Robbie slapped her a high five.

I'm sunk, Michelle thought. No way are these little monsters going to let me teach them anything!

Now she knew *exactly* how Mr. Kowalski felt. These three kids just played sink the sub with *her*. And they won!

Chapter

8

❤ Michelle watch her father flip one of his special burgers on the outdoor grill. The whole family was getting ready for dinner in the backyard.

"I didn't get a chance to ask you how it went in school yesterday," Danny said.

Joey came down the back steps with an armload of mustard, ketchup, and pickles. "Yeah, Michelle. What happened? Did you sink the sub?"

Danny turned around and glanced from Joey to Michelle. "Sink the sub? I don't like the sound of that. What exactly went on with your substitute?"

Michelle sighed. Then she told her family about the pranks they played on Mr. Kowalski. And what happened when Mr. Kowalski put her and Lee in charge of the class.

Danny shook his head. "Michelle—"

Stephanie jabbed D.J. in the ribs. "Watch out. Here comes Dad Talk Number Thirty-seven."

"I remember that one," D.J. answered.

"You know better than to misbehave in school," her father continued. "What a rough day for that poor substitute teacher! How did you come up with the idea to play tricks on him anyway? D.J. and Stephanie never—"

"Umm . . ." Joey began.

"Well . . . we did tell her about some of the silly stuff we did in school," Jesse said.

"I should have known," Danny said.

"We didn't mean to get Michelle in trouble," Jesse told him.

"You didn't," Danny answered. "I'm not happy you told her those stories. But *she* got herself in trouble."

Danny looked Michelle in the eye. "The fact that Joey and Jesse used to play sink the sub doesn't make it right. You have to think for yourself."

"But Lee is the one who set the alarm on my watch. That part wasn't really my fault! But that's why Mr. Kowalski made me teach the class," Michelle explained.

Her father frowned.

"Okay, okay. I should have asked Lee what he planned to do with my watch. And I shouldn't have done any of the other stuff either," she admitted. "Things started happening, and everybody joined in. It seemed like fun at the time."

"That's what I'm trying to tell you,"

Danny said firmly. "You can't just go along with the crowd."

Michelle nodded. Then she told her family about her new assignment to teach the second-graders spelling. She imitated Robbie, Alan, and Claire. "Robbie just stared at me and told me they didn't have to do what I said. It was horrible!" Michelle concluded.

Everyone cracked up. Even her dad.

"It's not funny!" Michelle exclaimed.

"You're right, honey," Danny said. He scooped the burgers off the grill and brought them to the picnic table.

Aunt Becky tucked napkins into the twins' shirts. "Maybe we can help," she said.

"Really?" Michelle said. "How?"

"We can brainstorm and come up with some good ideas to help you teach your students, and make them listen," she answered. "If we all put our heads together,

I'm sure we'll come up with something good."

"Great!" Michelle ran upstairs and got her notebook. Then she ran back outside and took her place at the table. "Okay—shoot!" she said.

Everybody started talking at once. That happened a lot in Michelle's full house.

"Hold it, hold it!" Danny hollered. "Stephanie, why don't you start. Then we'll go around the table."

"Bribe them with candy," Stephanie suggested. "That's what I do when I baby-sit."

"Any special kind?" Michelle asked.

Stephanie thought hard. "M&Ms usually work. Almost all kids like them—and they aren't messy."

Michelle wrote that down.

"Your turn, D.J.," Danny said.

"My advice?" D.J. said. "Quit. Tell your teacher you give up."

"D.J.!" Danny exclaimed. He leaned across the table toward her. "What have I always taught you girls? Tanners are not quitters! Quitting is not the solution to anything."

"But those kids will never listen to Michelle," D.J. argued. "They are too close to her own age. You have to be at least five years older for kids to listen to you. That's what I found out when I used to baby-sit."

"But I can't give up," Michelle moaned. "My whole class is counting on me." She thought about Jeff. Well, almost my whole class.

"That's right," her father said.

"My turn," Joey called out. "Tell them jokes—try to be their pal."

"Just don't tell them any of Joey's jokes. That will really make them cry," Jesse teased.

"I think you're all wrong," Danny said

as he passed around his special low-fat coleslaw. "Michelle, why not try explaining to them why spelling is important? Make them *want* to learn to spell."

Michelle scribbled notes as fast as she could. Her family had so many ideas—all different. One of them had to work, right?

I'm going to do it, Michelle told herself. I'm going to teach those little kids to spell every word on the list Miss Strickland gave me!

She smoothed down the skirt of her navy blue jumper. It wasn't her favorite. She liked brighter colors, and she usually wore jeans or leggings to school.

But she thought the jumper made her look older—and if D.J. was right, looking older might help her get the kids to pay attention.

The door opened, and Robbie, Alan, and Claire burst inside.

Before she could say a word, Robbie grabbed Michelle's spelling book and tossed it behind a filing cabinet. It took her five minutes to fish it out.

Michelle didn't yell. She calmly opened her backpack and pulled out a jumbo bag of M&Ms. She shook the bag in their faces. "Spell a word right, and I'll give you an M&M."

"Just one?" Robbie complained. "One little candy? That's not even worth trying for."

"Yeah," Alan agreed.

"How about two?" Michelle bargained.

The kids shook their heads.

"Five?" Michelle was starting to get worried.

"How about the whole bag!" Robbie snatched the bag from her hand and ripped it open. He stuffed a handful of candy into his mouth. "Look at me," he mumbled through the candy. "I can spell M&M!"

"Give that back!" Michelle grabbed for the bag. Robbie jerked it out of reach— and M&Ms flew over the floor.

Alan and Claire lunged for the spilled candy. "Don't eat off the floor," Michelle ordered. "I'll get blamed if you get sick. Get some clean candy from Robbie."

Michelle picked up the M&Ms, took a deep breath, and started in again. She tried everything.

She put frowny faces next to their names when they acted up.

She explained to them why they needed to know how to spell.

She tried giving them easy words to build up their confidence.

Nothing worked. She was feeling desperate. "Did you hear about the kid who got a pack of gum for his little brother?" Michelle asked.

"Huh?" Robbie stared at her.

Michelle grinned. At least that got his attention. "Yeah. Sounded like a good swap to me," she answered.

None of the kids laughed. "It's a joke," Michelle explained.

Alan frowned. "I don't get it."

"Me neither," Claire said.

"You know," Michelle answered. "The kid didn't *buy* some gum for his little brother, he *traded*—"

"I got it," Robbie said. "But it's not funny."

Jesse told me not to use one of Joey's jokes, Michelle thought. Boy was he right!

After dinner that night, Michelle headed up to her room. She felt exhausted. And she still hadn't come up with any new ideas for teaching the kids to spell.

Tomorrow is my last chance, she

thought. Their spelling test is in the afternoon.

When she got to the second floor, she could hear the twins singing in the bathtub. Songs they learned at preschool.

Michelle laughed. They were totally off key. But they made up for it by turning up the volume!

The twins were singing the old alphabet song. The same one Michelle had learned when she was little. "A, B, C, D, E, F, G . . ."

Wow! Michelle thought. They remember all the letters, and they are only four.

Michelle climbed the stairs to the third floor so she could hear better. The twins launched into another song:

"There was a farmer had a dog
And Bingo was his name-o
B-I-N-G-O
B-I-N-G-O

B-I-N-G-O
And Bingo was his name-o"

Michelle ran into the bathroom.

Aunt Becky knelt by the tub. She scrubbed the singing twins as they splashed in the water. "Hi, Michelle. What's up?" she asked. She brushed a wet strand of hair off her face.

"I wanted to say thanks to Nicky and Alex! They just gave me the most amazing idea!"

"You're welcome!" Nicky chirped.

"You're welcome!" Alex echoed.

Michelle turned around and dashed downstairs. She had a ton of work to do before bedtime.

Would her idea work? Would she finally be able to teach those little monsters to spell?

Chapter 9

♥ Michelle wasn't trying to look older today. She had on her funkiest outfit. She wore her long light blue sweatshirt over pink polka-dot leggings. Her pink high tops with scrunched white socks. Her pink and blue baseball cap—on backward. And a pair of sunglasses.

When Claire, Alan, and Robbie trooped in for their tutoring session, they started to giggle.

I might not look like a regular teacher, she thought. But watch out! I'm ready to teach.

Michelle pulled the boom box she borrowed from Stephanie out of her backpack. She slipped in the special cassette tape she recorded the night before. She pushed the play button, and music filled the room. Loud music. *Ba-BOOM, ba-BOOM, ba-BOOM.*

This better work, she thought. It's my last chance.

The three kids glanced at each other. "Are you sure it's okay to play that in here?" Claire asked.

"Won't we get in trouble?" Alan asked.

"Are you *nuts?*" Robbie demanded.

"Nope," Michelle said, and she started to move to the music. "I'm a spelling ace getting in the groove. Listen up.

"Put me to the test
A spelling test.
'Cause I'm the best
Better than the rest."

The kids stared at her as if she were from another planet. Uh-oh, she thought. Did I goof again?

Hang in there, Michelle, she told herself. And keep singing!

"BANANA!

Yo! Don't yell it!
I can spell it!
B-A-N-A-N-A—hey!
Had one in my lunch today."

On the second verse, Claire began to clap and sway.

By the third verse, Robbie and Alan were humming along.

When Michelle finished, she had used every word on the kids' spelling list in her song. Michelle pushed the stop button. "Well, what do you guys think?"

Claire looked at Alan.

Alan looked at Robbie.

Robbie stared at Michelle.

Then they all started clapping. Claire whistled through her teeth.

Michelle couldn't stop smiling. They liked it!

"Wow, Michelle!" Robbie exclaimed. "That was awesome! Where did you find that song?"

"I made it up," Michelle said.

"Really?" Alan asked. "All by yourself?"

Michelle nodded. "Uh-huh."

"You made it up for us?" Claire asked softly, twirling a strand of her dark hair. "Even though we were mean to you?"

"Yep. My twin cousins gave me the idea," she explained. "I heard them singing 'Bingo' in the bathtub. They knew how to spell the word *bingo,* even though they are only four years old."

"I know that song too!" Alan said.

" 'B-I-N-G-O, and Bingo was his name-o.' "

"See? You *can* spell," Michelle told him.

"Well, it's easy when it's a song," Alan answered.

"Yeah," Claire agreed. "Singing is fun. I love to sing. I want to be a rock star when I grow up."

"Well, rock stars need to know how to spell too," Michelle said. "Mrs. Yoshida, my fourth-grade teacher, always tries to make things interesting and fun. We usually have a good time in her class. That makes even the tough stuff seem easier."

"I hope I get her when I'm in fourth grade," Claire said. "She sounds cool."

"So, what do you think?" Michelle asked. "Do you want to try out my song and see if it helps you on your spelling test this afternoon? It will be fun."

"Yes!" All three of Michelle's students yelled.

"*Don't* sit down. And *don't* be quiet," she instructed. She had the three kids join her in the front of the room and gave them each copies of the song's words. Then she pressed the start button.

Michelle felt more and more nervous as the day went on. Were her kids finished with their spelling test? How did they do? When would she know?

I'll probably have to wait until after school, Michelle thought. We don't have another recess today. And I doubt Miss Strickland will come over and tell me.

"Earth to Michelle! Earth to Michelle! Come in, Michelle!" a voice called.

"Huh?"

Mr. Kowalski grinned at her. "The question was, how many days does it take for the moon to travel around the earth. You seemed to be on the moon, so I thought you could tell us," he teased.

Michelle felt her face get hot as the class laughed along with their sub.

"I know what's on your mind, Michelle," Mr. Kowalski added. "Why don't you go across the hall and ask Miss Strickland how your kids did on their test."

"Thanks!" Michelle exclaimed. She jumped up and bolted over to Miss Strickland's room.

Then she took a deep breath—and opened the door. "Excuse me," she said to Miss Strickland. "Mr. Kowalski said I could come over and see how the spelling test went."

I hope she has good news! Michelle thought. She crossed her fingers.

"Come in," Miss Strickland called.

Miss *Strict*-land actually sounds a little friendly, Michelle thought.

"All three of the students you tutored

made A's on their tests," Miss Strickland told her. "I was so amazed. Robbie made a hundred. And Alan and Claire missed only one each."

Michelle scanned the class for Robbie. He was blushing. But Michelle could tell he was super proud of himself.

Claire grinned at Michelle from the next row.

And Alan gave her a big thumbs-up from his desk by the window.

"I'm impressed you were able to hold their attention. You must have a talent for keeping order."

"Uh, not really," Michelle admitted.

Miss Strickland raised her eyebrows. "Then what is your secret?" she asked.

Michelle couldn't believe it. Miss Strickland wanted her advice—on teaching.

"I made up a song with all twenty of their spelling words in it. When they learned the song—they learned to spell!" Michelle explained.

"Now I know why Claire kept humming during the test," Miss Strickland said with a laugh.

Michelle laughed too. Then she waved to Robbie, Alan, and Claire and headed back across the hall to her room.

"Well?" Lee demanded the moment she opened the door.

"They all got A's!" Michelle cried.

A bunch of cheers—and a couple of loud boos from Jeff—filled the room.

"Way to go, Michelle!" Cassie called.

"You did a great job this week," Mr. Kowalski said as Michelle took her seat.

"Thanks," Michelle said. "It was a *lot* harder than I thought it would be. But it was fun too."

"I learned something from you too," Mr. Kowalski told her.

"From Michelle? Maybe you should go back to college, Mr. K.," Jeff joked.

"When we switched places, I remembered what it's like to be a kid," Mr. Kowalski explained. "I hope I'll always remember that. I think it will make me a better teacher. And I know I'll be a lot better prepared when my students try to 'sink the sub.' "

Mr. Kowalski picked up the stack of spelling tests from the corner of his desk. "Now, about these tests. I'm going to call this batch a practice test and let everyone take the test again."

"You did it, Michelle!" Mandy called.

"Please put your *real* names on the test this time," Mr. Kowalski instructed. "Okay, Anna Abdul?" he asked, smiling at Michelle.

Michelle tore a sheet of clean paper out of her notebook and got ready for the first word.

Beep-beep. Beep-beep. Beep-beep.

Oh, no! This can't be happening again, Michelle thought. At least it wasn't her watch beeping this time.

"I guess we'll have to take the test after recess," Mr. Kowalski said.

What? They didn't have another recess today!

Kids starting crowding toward the door.

Michelle pushed her away over to Mr. Kowalski. "Uh, you know we aren't supposed to have another recess, right?" she asked quietly.

"Michelle, the beeping sound means recess. Everybody knows that," he answered. He held out his arm so she could tell it was *his* watch beeping and grinned at her.

"You're the teacher!" Michelle answered.

It doesn't matter if you live around the corner...
or around the world...
If you are a fan of Mary-Kate and Ashley Olsen,
you should be a member of

MARY-KATE + ASHLEY'S FUN CLUB™

Here's what you get:
Our Funzine™
An autographed color photo
Two black & white individual photos
A full size color poster
An official **Fun Club™** membership card
A **Fun Club™** school folder
Two special **Fun Club™** surprises
A holiday card
Fun Club™ collectibles catalog
Plus a **Fun Club™** box to keep everything in

To join Mary-Kate + Ashley's Fun Club™, fill out the form
below and send it along with

U.S. Residents – $17.00
Canadian Residents – $22 U.S. Funds
International Residents – $27 U.S. Funds

MARY-KATE + ASHLEY'S FUN CLUB™
859 HOLLYWOOD WAY, SUITE 275
BURBANK, CA 91505

NAME:_____

ADDRESS:_____

_CITY:_____ STATE:_____ ZIP:_____

PHONE:(____) _____ BIRTHDATE:_____

FULL HOUSE™
Michelle

#1: THE GREAT PET PROJECT 51905-0/$3.50

#2: THE SUPER-DUPER SLEEPOVER PARTY 51906-9/$3.50

#3: MY TWO BEST FRIENDS 52271-X/$3.99

#4: LUCKY, LUCKY DAY 52272-8/$3.50

#5: THE GHOST IN MY CLOSET 53573-0/$3.99

#6: BALLET SURPRISE 53574-9/$3.99

#7: MAJOR LEAGUE TROUBLE 53575-7/$3.99

#8: MY FOURTH-GRADE MESS 53576-5/$3.99

#9: BUNK 3, TEDDY, AND ME 56834-5/$3.99

#10: MY BEST FRIEND IS A MOVIE STAR! (Super Edition) 56835-3/$3.99

#11: THE BIG TURKEY ESCAPE 56836-1/$3.99

#12: THE SUBSTITUTE TEACHER 00364-X/$3.99

#13: CALLING ALL PLANETS 00365-8/$3.50

#14: I'VE GOT A SECRET 00366-6/$3.99

#15: HOW TO BE COOL 00833-1/$3.99

A MINSTREL® BOOK

Published by Pocket Books

Simon & Schuster Mail Order Dept. BWB
200 Old Tappan Rd., Old Tappan, N.J. 07675

Please send me the books I have checked above. I am enclosing $_____(please add $0.75 to cover the postage and handling for each order. Please add appropriate sales tax). Send check or money order--no cash or C.O.D.'s please. Allow up to six weeks for delivery. For purchase over $10.00 you may use VISA: card number, expiration date and customer signature must be included.

Name _____

Address _____

City _____ State/Zip _____

VISA Card # _____ Exp.Date _____

Signature _____

1033-19

FULL HOUSE™
Stephanie

PHONE CALL FROM A FLAMINGO	88004-7/$3.99
THE BOY-OH-BOY NEXT DOOR	88121-3/$3.99
TWIN TROUBLES	88290-2/$3.99
HIP HOP TILL YOU DROP	88291-0/$3.99
HERE COMES THE BRAND NEW ME	89858-2/$3.99
THE SECRET'S OUT	89859-0/$3.99
DADDY'S NOT-SO-LITTLE GIRL	89860-4/$3.99
P.S. FRIENDS FOREVER	89861-2/$3.99
GETTING EVEN WITH THE FLAMINGOES	52273-6/$3.99
THE DUDE OF MY DREAMS	52274-4/$3.99
BACK-TO-SCHOOL COOL	52275-2/$3.99
PICTURE ME FAMOUS	52276-0/$3.99
TWO-FOR-ONE CHRISTMAS FUN	53546-3/$3.99
THE BIG FIX-UP MIX-UP	53547-1/$3.99
TEN WAYS TO WRECK A DATE	53548-X/$3.99
WISH UPON A VCR	53549-8/$3.99
DOUBLES OR NOTHING	56841-8/$3.99
SUGAR AND SPICE ADVICE	56842-6/$3.99
NEVER TRUST A FLAMINGO	56843-4/$3.99
THE TRUTH ABOUT BOYS	00361-5/$3.99
CRAZY ABOUT THE FUTURE	00362-3/$3.99

Available from Minstrel® Books Published by Pocket Books

Simon & Schuster Mail Order Dept. BWB
200 Old Tappan Rd., Old Tappan, N.J. 07675

Please send me the books I have checked above. I am enclosing $_____(please add $0.75 to cover the postage and handling for each order. Please add appropriate sales tax). Send check or money order--no cash or C.O.D.'s please. Allow up to six weeks for delivery. For purchase over $10.00 you may use VISA: card number, expiration date and customer signature must be included.

Name _____

Address _____

City _____ State/Zip _____

VISA Card # _____ Exp.Date _____

Signature _____

929-19